DISCARD

The Great Butterfly Hunt

The Mystery of the Migrating Monarchs

Ethan Herberman

Simon and Schuster Books for Young Readers
Published by Simon & Schuster Inc., New York

In association with WGBH Boston,
producers of NOVA for public television

SIMON AND SCHUSTER
BOOKS FOR YOUNG READERS
Simon & Schuster Building
Rockefeller Center
1230 Avenue of the Americas
New York, New York 10020

Manufactured in the United
States of America.

10 9 8 7 6 5 4 3 2 1
10 9 8 7 6 5 4 3 2 1 (pbk.)

Library of Congress
Cataloging-in-Publication Data
Herberman, Ethan.
     The Great Butterfly Hunt: the
     Mystery of the Migrating Monarchs/
Ethan Herberman.
     (A NOVABOOK)
     "In association with WGBH
Boston, producers of NOVA for
public television."
     Includes index.
     Summary: Examines the migration
patterns of the monarch butterfly,
describes the study and discoveries that
yielded knowledge of these movements,
and speculates on the origin of the insect
and why it travels such long distances.
     1. Monarch butterfly – juvenile
literature. [1. Monarch butterfly.
2. Butterflies.] I. WGBH (Television
station: Boston, Mass.) II. Title. III. Series.
QL561.D3H47 1990
595.78'9 – dc20
90-31571 CIP AC

ISBN 0-671-69427-8
ISBN 0-671-69428-6 (pbk.)

Cover:
**A monarch butterfly soars
aloft. The monarch got its
name from English settlers in
North America. They looked
at its brightly colored wings
and thought of William of
Orange, their king, or monarch.**

The Great Butterfly Hunt
is dedicated to the Great
Butterfly Hunters. Their curiosity uncovered one of nature's
most beautiful secrets.

Among the many monarch
finders and taggers who
helped make this book possible, I owe special thanks to
Jo Brewer, Ken and Cathy
Brugger, Margaret Elliott,
Nancy Hoeflich, Jim Gilbert,
Jim Street, John McClusky,
Clara Waterman, and
Audrey Wilson.
     At WGBH, I am indebted
to the many talented people in
the publishing and design de-
partments. Many thanks as
well to the Simon and
Schuster Children's Book
Division; to photo researcher
Elise Katz; to William Calvert
and Juan Merkt, who re-
viewed the manuscript; and to
the other scientists who en-
riched it with their expertise,
among them Lincoln Brower,
Julian Donahue, John Fales,
Stephen Malcolm, Ian Nisbet,
Simon Perkins, Klaus Schmidt-
Koenig, and Charles Walcott.
     And thanks, finally, to my
folks, Harry and Susan
Herberman, for unflagging
encouragement and support.

The NOVA television series is
produced by WGBH Boston.
NOVA is made possible by
the Johnson & Johnson Family
of Companies, Lockheed, and
public television viewers.

Right:
**Traveling in vast numbers,
monarchs have long
caused people to wonder:
Where are these insects
headed? And why?**

Contents

The Mountain's Secret

The first clue appeared shortly after daybreak on January 2, 1975. Standing on a deserted roadside, Ken Brugger looked up and saw a lone monarch butterfly soaring down from the mountain called Cerro Pelón.

To most people, such a sight would have meant little. But to Ken Brugger, an American explorer in south-central Mexico, it meant a lot. Monarchs don't fly in the dark, so this one must have spent the night on the mountain. Ken turned to his wife, Cathy. Perhaps *now* they would have some success.

Then, for the fourteenth time in fourteen days, Ken and Cathy Brugger set out for the peak.

Soon they would be climbing through the thick forest that covered Cerro Pelón almost to its rocky summit. But first they had to cross the patchwork of farms and villages that circled the mountain's base, and this was the most dangerous part of the trek. On the morning of their third climb, for instance, a farmer had cornered them on an exposed hillside. "If you are looking for treasure," he said, "my friends and I will get our guns. We'll come after you." Before their ninth climb, a dozen men armed with carbine rifles had threatened them again.

Nevertheless, they refused to stay away. They wore extra-thick, homemade blue jeans as protection against snakes and broad-brimmed white hats to protect against the sun. Ken carried a .32-caliber automatic pistol in a specially sewn pocket of his shirt.

Were they really after treasure? Some might have said so. It was not, to be sure, the treasure in the mind of the farmer. (Legend had it that the famed revolutionary general Emiliano Zapata had stashed a priceless hoard in just that region of the mountains.) But it was treasure all the same. And, what's more, the Bruggers knew they were close to finding it at about noon on that fourteenth day.

That was when they discovered the wings – wings that looked like stained-glass windows. They found them on the ground – at first one, then three, then seven. . . . And by the time they had climbed up into the clouds, they were finding monarch bodies, too. Pecked at by birds, these lay strewn about, still waiting for the mice and other scavengers that would soon hasten to carry them away.

Their hearts pounding, the Bruggers climbed on. They advanced as quickly as possible through the mountain's steep forest, scrambled over loose stones, waded through dense tangles of undergrowth. Then, suddenly Cathy saw it: a butterfly . . . alive in spite of the cold . . . way up there! They moved even faster, silent, breathless, almost reaching the topmost limit of the forest before the trail of wings curved away to a small grove where they heard a rustling that wasn't the wind, and the day grew dark, although not because of the trees.

The Bruggers could not speak. In the past, thousands of people had tried to find what was hidden on that mountain. But of all these searchers, Ken and Cathy were the first to discover its secret. Eventually, Cathy lay down. Just to see what would happen, she stretched out on the forest floor, and the monarchs covered her, one by one, with their shimmering, trembling wings.

The search was over. The treasure was found.

The Journey Begins

Driven by instinct, this butterfly is on its way through a city. When faced with obstacles like bridges and buildings, migrating monarchs will fly right over them, even when they can take an easier way around.

Months before, the great monarch journey had begun.

It had been going on every spring and fall for thousands of years. It continues today.

Perhaps you have seen it.

If you live on the Gulf coast of Texas, for instance, you may have watched as hundreds of monarch butterflies poured across a highway, a fluttering caravan that may have taken hours to pass.

If you live in Manhattan, you may have seen the monarchs. Out of a high window, you may have watched as several confronted an office tower, then flew upward, higher and higher, until they surged over it instead of taking the easy way around.

And if you live near Cape May, New Jersey, or Eastern Point, Massachusetts, or Point Pelee, Ontario, you may have seen the butterflies, too. In these locations and others like them, land juts southward into large lakes and bays that the monarchs must cross. But sometimes they can't. So people who visit such places on exactly the right late-summer or autumn mornings are in for a surprise. They find that the dead leaves that seem to be hanging from certain trees are actually butterflies – thousands and thousands of butterflies. Draped on a bed of boughs, the insects cloak the trees in the dull colors of their closed wings: tans and browns.

It's a good idea to keep watch, though. In a single instant as sunlight pours into the grove, the butterflies repaint the trees in the color of their opening wings: a dazzling orange-and-black. Then, within the hour, they're up from the trunks and branches – rising, hovering, swooping, swirling. All the while they are waiting for the right wind change, the right temperature increase – the right change in weather that will send them on their way.

Only then do they head out over the water. Beforehand they wait, hunting flower nectar by day, hanging off the trees by night. Their numbers swell as more and more arrive to join those already in the grove. Eventually, though, the trees lose their many-colored butterfly coat. The weather improves. The monarchs depart.

On their way again, they may cover as many as eighty miles (129 km) in a day, flying at speeds as great as twenty miles (32 km) per hour and at heights of two miles (3.2 km). And all the while, they are racing southwest – farther and farther southwest – across the central and eastern expanses of Canada and the United States.

Why aren't these butterflies migrating? For some reason, they have bunched together on Cape May, New Jersey. There they wait – sipping nectar from wild flowers – until better weather allows them to continue on their way.

Every autumn, kids in Pacific Grove, California, march in a parade to celebrate the arrival of countless monarchs. The butterflies come from colder regions west of the Rocky Mountains to spend the winter clustered in trees along the California coast.

Destination Unknown

But southwest to *where*? Before 1975, no one knew. Monarchs west of the Rocky Mountains had long been thought to spend their winters in California. There, millions would crowd yearly onto the same familiar trees, waiting, it seemed, until warmer weather permitted a return to more northerly or mountainous haunts. But how about the rest – those hundreds of millions of monarchs that flourished each summer east of the Rocky Mountains, from the Canadian provinces in the north to Florida in the south?

Every fall they just seemed to disappear.

Did they, too, have a winter home? If so, why had nobody reported it? And if they did have one, how did they find it? How did they know when to go there? Did they make a round trip? Did they migrate as birds do? . . .

To *migrate* means to travel from one place to another in search of better living conditions or a place to reproduce. Pacific salmon migrate, for instance, when they make their once-in-a-lifetime journey upstream to mate and lay eggs in the shallows where they hatched. Microscopic sea animals migrate when they rise to the surface, as they do every evening, to feed.

To say that creatures migrate "as birds do," however, means something more exact, for most migrating birds repeat a specific two-way journey year after year. At a set time, they gather together in flocks and head south to escape winter; then, as winter ends, they return north to breed. In these migrations they may cross whole continents; nevertheless, they find their way to almost exactly the same locations – perhaps even to the same trees – they occupied the previous year.

Some animals migrate every year, but others make a once-in-a-lifetime journey. These salmon, for instance, have left the Pacific Ocean and are swimming upstream in Canada to the freshwater shallows where they hatched. There they will mate, lay eggs, and die.

Coping with Hard Times

Short days, scarce food, killing cold – that's winter. Animals confront it in a number of ways. Some, like city squirrels, store food. Others, like woodchucks, reduce their need to eat by hibernating. When woodchucks *hibernate*, they roll themselves up and almost shut themselves down. They breathe as little as once every five minutes. Nearly frozen, they leave on only a "pilot light" of life to preserve them until spring.

Other animals follow a third course. They escape from winter by migrating to warmer climates and returning only when the whole troublesome season has passed.

As summer ends, many species are beginning such seasonal, two-way migrations. Herds of caribou are walking from the treeless arctic Barren Grounds to more southerly forests. Pods of gray whales are swimming from the coast of Alaska to the coast of California, where they breed. Of all these travelers, however, those we know best are the birds. About one-third of the world's birds migrate, and in the north you can see the signs of their departure everywhere – in hundreds of swallows lining telephone wires, in V-shaped flocks of Canada geese honking noisily through the sky. . . .

That so many travel in groups, points to a key fact about migration: It's dangerous. In fact, it is so dangerous that, according to some experts, more than half of all migrating birds die before completing their first round trip.

In crossing unknown territory, an animal risks starving, getting eaten, or losing its way. By grouping together, on the other hand, each migrant betters its chances of finishing the journey safely. The many members of a group looking for food can search out a large area. What's more, a migrant among others of its kind is far safer from enemies than a migrant alone.

Most important, the group often includes older, experienced individuals that remember the route and can show the others the way.

Do monarchs travel in groups? At least one scientist says they might. He suggests, for example, that when a migrating monarch lands on a tree and spreads its wings, this is an invitation for others to join it.

But other scientists disagree. They say the butterflies show no signs of cooperating and only end up together by accident, when winds and landforms (like valleys and mountains) funnel them into the same places at the same times.

Migrants need not swim or fly. Caribou walk back and forth between the forests and the treeless tundra of the far north.

Migrating in a flock helps these Canada Geese locate food and escape predators. Traveling with older birds helps younger ones find their way.

Such feats prove hard enough to explain when a robin, barn swallow, or Canada goose is performing them. Now imagine a butterfly doing exactly the same thing. It scarcely seems possible. For one thing, butterflies lack the size and sturdiness of birds, so how could they travel thousands of miles? For another, they cannot possibly benefit from experience, as birds do. Birds, after all, will often migrate in the company of older birds that have flown the route before. But monarchs can have no such teachers since none lives long enough to migrate twice.

So how would they find their way? Clearly, they would have to rely on *instinct*. In other words, they would have to be born with the ability to stay on course over hundreds or even thousands of miles. It is hardly surprising, then, that some scientists have refused to believe that monarchs make long, two-way migrations and instead have suggested that the butterflies survive northern winters without going anywhere. Perhaps, they have theorized, the adult butterflies hibernate under logs, like mourning cloak butterflies. Or maybe they all perish but leave behind eggs or caterpillars that survive.

In fact, the mystery of the monarchs' great voyage might never have been solved had it not been for the efforts of a single determined scientist and thousands of volunteers.

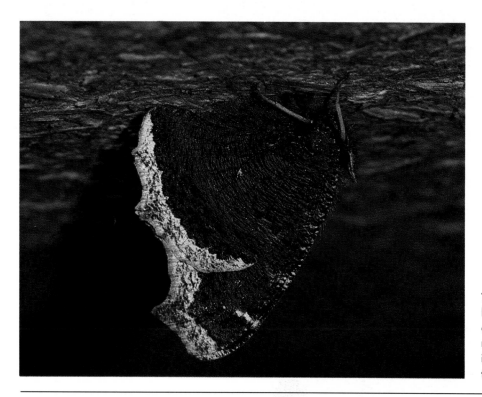

This mourning cloak butterfly was found hibernating under a board, upside down. Some scientists used to think that monarchs hibernate, too. The idea of insects migrating like birds was simply too hard for them to believe.

Marvelous Monarchs

To be sure, some of these people were also scientists, but most were not. They were lawyers, teachers, shopkeepers, housewives – ordinary people who made important contributions to a major scientific find, sometimes without leaving their backyards! Nor were they all adults. Lots of kids participated. In fact, kids made some of the biggest contributions of all.

As for the scientist who led the volunteers, his name is Fred A. Urquhart, and he is a world famous *entomologist* – a scientist who studies insects. Now retired as a university professor, Urquhart still lives in Toronto, the Canadian city from which he launched the Great Butterfly Hunt in 1935, at the age of twenty-three. Together with his wife, Norah, he has spent much of his life since then studying monarch butterflies. He has driven thousands of miles in search of them, written books about them and even eaten one or two in the interest of science.

Antenna   Front Wing
Head   Eye
Thorax   Rear Wing
Abdomen   Alar Spot (Male Only)

Spectacular wings that span three to four inches (7.6 to 10.2 cm) make the monarch one of the most beautiful of butterflies. Like all insects, it has six legs and a body divided into head, thorax and abdomen. And, like all insects, it is cold-blooded: Its temperature rises and falls with that of the surrounding air. Notice the "alar" spots on the back wings. Only males have these markings.

◄

Fred Urquhart with his wife, Norah, in 1957. Though he had been studying the eastern monarchs for twenty-two years, he still had no idea where they went.

In summer, North American monarchs may turn up as far north as James Bay, but most live in the areas shaded on the map above. Notice that the Rocky Mountains split the monarchs into eastern and western populations.

Yet Urquhart's interest is not all that difficult to understand, for even apart from their mass migrations, these colorful creatures are exciting and enticing, as dazzling to the mind as they are to the eye. Consider the following monarch facts:

• Of all the many kinds, or *species*, of butterflies similar to them, only monarchs have spread outside the world's hot zones. They're tropical animals, like alligators and pythons, and yet during warmer months they're found as far away from the tropics as James Bay in Canada. Like the other butterflies that are similar to them, however, monarchs cannot withstand freezing cold. Neither can their eggs nor developing young. If exposed to the freezing cold of a northern winter, a monarch at any stage of its life will quickly die.

• You will seldom find a monarch where you do not also find some species of milkweed. The reason is simple: Milkweed leaves are the only food that monarch caterpillars will eat. Destroy the world's milkweeds, therefore, and you destroy the world's monarchs. Watch over milkweed, on the other hand, and you may someday be rewarded with the sight of a monarch mother curling the tip of her abdomen and laying a single jewel-like egg on the underside of a leaf.

• Monarchs transform themselves before your eyes. They undergo a spectacular *metamorphosis*, or change of body. True, many insects

From Egg to Adult: The Life Cycle of the Monarch

1 An adult monarch female lays a speck-sized egg on the underside of a milkweed leaf.

2 Within days, the *larva*, or caterpillar, hatches and begins to eat. It eats so much milkweed that its skin splits open four times; and each time, out comes the caterpillar, wearing a roomier skin, to feed anew.

3 Now some two inches (5 cm) long and 3,000 times its birth weight, the two-week-old caterpillar is ready for the biggest change of all.

4 With silk that comes from a gland below its jaws, the mature caterpillar spins a silk button on the underside of some object, then hangs from it by its back legs and waits.

experience metamorphosis. Maggots become flies, grubs become beetles. But few do it in such a splendid way.

Notice what happens to the caterpillar in the pictures at the bottom of the page. First, it hangs down. Then, it seems to split open. Its skin falls off. A chrysalis (also called a *pupa*) remains. At least, that's what a scientist would call it. In fact, a chrysalis looks like a lantern crafted of brilliant jade and studded with golden gems.

For a week, maybe more, the chrysalis hangs motionless. But don't let its stillness fool you. It only looks like a lifeless jewel. Inside, rapid change is taking place. A butterfly is growing while a caterpillar is disappearing. Cells in the caterpillar's own blood are eating it away.

What is metamorphosis like? Well, you might compare it to starting your life as a person, then growing a shell and emerging as a bird. Indeed, what happens to monarchs seems no stranger than that. But what happens to some monarchs is stranger still. Just as the adult butterfly is different from the caterpillar, so, too, the butterfly that hatches from its chrysalis in late summer or early fall is different from the butterfly that hatched only weeks before. Scientists aren't certain what causes this difference. They think it's the cooler temperatures of autumn and the rapidly shortening days. Whatever the cause, however, the effect is obvious.

Once again, as we shall see, the monarch has changed.

Does this plant remind you of monarchs? It should. Found on roadsides and in fields, common milkweed (and its relatives) provides the monarch caterpillar's only food.

5 Hours pass. Once again its skin splits. A black hook reaches out. It grabs the silk button. Meanwhile, the caterpillar's legs, mouth, and antennae start falling away, along with the skin.

6 What remains is the chrysalis, or pupa. Notice the faint outline of a butterfly in its surface, the gold spots, still mysterious, that line its face.

7 In about ten days, the chrysalis becomes as clear as sandwich wrap, revealing the butterfly that has been developing within. Do you want to see it hatch? Then don't look away, not even for eighty seconds, because on average . . .

8 . . . that's all the time it needs. Hanging from its wrapper, the new butterfly must first pump fluid into its still-crumpled wings, then allow them to dry. In a few hours, it is ready to go, but where? That depends on where and when it hatched.

Tracking Autumn's Monarch

Quite unlike its parents, the autumn monarch spends little time in the region of its birth. Within hours, it is off and away – migrating almost constantly, feeding sometimes but stopping to rest only in bad weather and at night. Most likely it joins a stream of monarchs. The stream joins others; it becomes a river. Yet even when flying alone, the migrating butterfly will head for the same destination as all the others.

Storing fat is an important activity for the migrating monarchs of autumn. They need all the fuel they can get. You will therefore find them sipping nectar from many of the flowers they find along their routes – from milkweeds, asters, golden-rods, chrysanthemums, and more.

Take the time to watch monarchs – both nonmigrators in spring and summer and migrants in early fall – and you will notice several more differences between the two kinds. You will discover, for instance, that one may live seven, eight, or even twelve times as long as another! The spring and summer adults seem to speed through their life cycles. Within about four weeks, they have hatched from their chrysalises, fed, mated, laid eggs (if females), and died. The migrants, by contrast, live on and on. They actually become quite ancient, for butterflies, and in the safety of a rearing cage have astonished their keepers by clinging to life for a year.

Outdoors you will spot differences, too. Suppose, for example, you saw two monarchs, one chasing the other. Flying in swift, tight circles, they were spiraling higher and higher. In such a case, you would probably be watching nonmigrating, summertime monarchs. And up close you would likely see that the pursuer was a male and that the other, a female, was leading him on a romantic chase. If he kept up with her, she might eventually lead him to a branch. If you disturbed the branch, the two would rise again – as one! Clasping the female, abdomen to abdomen, the male would lift her to safety as they continued to mate.

▲
Are these autumn migrants? Impossible. Flying in swift, tight circles, the male monarch chases the female higher and higher until she leads him to a branch, where they mate. Disturbed, the two rise together as one. Migrating monarchs, by contrast, neither court nor mate during their fall journeys. You'd never see them behaving as the ones above.

The autumn migrants, by contrast, do not mate – nor can they. A look inside their bodies would show you why. Through a microscope, you could see that their sex organs have not yet developed. For now, they are incapable of producing young.

Here's yet another difference between the two kinds of monarchs: You will never see a migrant attack a bird! Male monarchs in spring and summer *will* sometimes attack birds, just as they will attack blowing leaves, other species of butterflies, and other male monarchs. True, they have nothing to attack these opponents with, neither claws nor jaws nor poisonous sting. In fact, their bodies extend no longer than the beaks of some of the birds they attack. Nevertheless, an unwary sparrow or redwing blackbird straying into the wrong patch of field may be in for a surprise. The monarch considers that patch his own; and he is upon the intruder in an instant, startling it with wildly flapping wings, dazzling it into a confused retreat.

The migrants, on the other hand, behave in exactly the opposite way. Male or female, they claim no territory. Rather, they bunch together in uncountable numbers and seem to lose all interest in individual space.

Urquhart's Quest

If you wanted to find migrating monarchs during late summer and early fall, then, you would do well to seek out the places where they gather. In the last chapter, we mentioned a few such places – points of land that jut out into large bodies of water which the monarchs must cross. But these are not the only ones. Throughout much of the United States and southern

Are these migrants? Absolutely. Only migrating monarchs cluster in butterfly trees like the pine at left. For some reason, they choose the same trees as overnight roosting places year after year.

Canada, you could also look for autumn migrants feeding and fattening themselves amid clusters of wild flowers. Or, you could look for "butterfly trees." To do that, however, it would be best to combine your looking with asking, because there's no real way, except through experience, to tell which trees might be butterfly trees .

Without knowing where to look, you would have to wait until a crowd of monarchs arrived one autumn evening, then observe carefully where they settled down. Generally, you would find that they landed on a few particular trees (or maybe just one) while leaving all the neighboring trees alone. Those are the butterfly trees! No one knows exactly why the monarchs cluster together on the same trees season after season. Indeed, many trees would seem equally suitable as places to spend the night. We do know one thing for certain, though. All the monarchs on a butterfly tree are migrants. Every one.

You can well imagine Fred Urquhart's curiosity as he first gazed up at these monarch-laden trees more than half a century ago. There they were, dripping with migrants. And yet, all of those monarchs would soon be gone – their destination unknown.

How could he ever find out where they went?

By catching them? Dissecting them? Chasing them in a plane? As it happened, scientists even then had come up with a reliable way of tracing out the routes of wandering creatures. First, they captured one and identified it with a kind of marker – a band or a tag, for example. Then, when the animal was recaptured elsewhere, the marker revealed where it had come from and how long it had been on the move.

With this method, scientists had successfully uncovered the secrets of several well-known migrating birds. It was one thing, however, to strap a band onto a long-legged gull; it was quite another to label an insect. How could anyone possibly accomplish that? Somehow, he or she would have to place a recognizable marker on a flapping, featherweight scrap of life – without hurting it, without interfering with its ability to fly! Nevertheless, this is exactly what Fred Urquhart set out to do. He began experimenting in the late 1930s, and by the mid-1950s, he seemed to have the problem solved. It had taken him just under twenty years!

A less determined man might well have given up, and certainly Urquhart had reason to. On a morning in 1954, for example, Fred and his wife, Norah, returned to a stand of pines on the Monterey peninsula in California. The previous day they had tagged about one thousand monarchs roosting in those trees. That night it had rained; and when they returned, the butterflies were gone, although the tags were still there. Washed from one thousand wings, they littered the ground.

Unlike the monarch caterpillar, the monarch adult has no mouth. Instead, it has a tube, called a *proboscis*, which usually stays coiled beneath its head. When uncoiled, the proboscis is like a drinking straw. As shown here, the butterfly uses it to suck nectar out of flowers.

Tracking: The Next Generation

Hello. I am whale number 646, now swimming eastward in the Atlantic Ocean. I have just surfaced from my fourth dive of the afternoon, which lasted ten minutes and twenty seconds. I reached a maximum depth of 600 feet (183 m), where the temperature was forty-one degrees Fahrenheit (5 C).

Although simple tags enabled the Urquharts and their volunteers to solve the mystery of the monarch's disappearance, such tags can only accomplish so much. True, they allow scientists to identify a migrating animal, and they can then compare its condition at a number of different locations. Yet the tags reveal nothing about what happens to the animal in between.

Dr. Bruce Mate.

Using recent inventions, however, scientists have been able to learn as much about some migrants' day-to-day experiences as they would have if the creatures had actually spoken the words at left.

One such scientist, Dr. Bruce Mate of Oregon State University, has been studying a rare kind of whale, called a right whale, that lives in the North Atlantic Ocean. When Dr. Mate finds a right whale, he gets close to it in a small boat, then attaches something that looks like a soup can to the whale's blubber. But what a soup can! Inside lie sensors that record depth, wetness, and temperature; a computer chip that collects and stores this information; and a transmitter that turns it into radio waves and sends it into outer space.

Meanwhile, some 510 miles (821 km) above the whale, two desk-sized satellites are whirling around our planet. Called Tiros-N satellites, they receive information from dozens of migrating animals, then pass it along to ground stations on earth, which, in turn, pass it along to scientists like Dr. Mate.

Tiros-N Satellite

The system has flaws. The transmitter cannot send signals through water, for example. It must therefore wait for the whale to surface. And it can only send signals every few hours, while a satellite is passing overhead. Nevertheless, Dr. Mate believes such long-range tracking can reveal extraordinary details about migration. "We are trying to put our eyes and ears on the animal," he says, "so it can describe to us where it's going and why."

Other scientists seem to agree with this approach. The result: Polar bears, penguins, walruses, swans, and other creatures are now also wearing fancy electronic lockets – some of which transmit to satellites and others to radio receivers positioned nearer by.

Right Whale

Ground Station

Monarchs by Mail

Yet the solution to the tagging problem turned out to be so simple. Go into any grocery store and you can see it. Notice the price tags sticking snugly to the smooth, shiny glassware. In the end, it was this kind of tag that Urquhart used in his quest. He cut it about half an inch square. He folded it over the leading edge of the butterfly's right front wing. Such a tag could survive a rainstorm. Equally important, the butterfly could survive the tag. Furthermore, it was large enough to hold all the information a monarch finder needed to see.

Each tag bore a printed serial number and the words, "Send to Museum Toronto, Canada." When Urquhart attached a tag, he recorded the serial number along with details about the monarch tagged. When someone found the monarch, the information on the tag allowed him or her to mail it to the museum in Toronto where Urquhart was then employed. Referring to the serial number, the professor could then figure out many things about the captured monarch – mainly, how far and in which general direction it had flown.

Pressed onto a featherlight wing, this paper tag stays put without harming the monarch. The tags have carried various messages over the years. This one, for example, asks the finder to send the butterfly to the University of Toronto.

Nevertheless, the Urquharts could hardly expect a few labeled insects to reveal the secrets of monarch migration. After all, of the masses of butterflies that coursed through North America each season, millions followed routes that people rarely traveled, while millions more died along the way. They ended up drowned, frozen, eaten by predators (such as mice, praying mantises, and garden spiders) or, most commonly, dashed to pieces by cars. What then were the chances of a tagged monarch catching the attention of some friendly finder, even if the Urquharts went out every year and tagged as many as they could?

The chances were slim, indeed.

The Urquharts needed help, and lots of it. With this in mind, Fred wrote an article for a well-known nature magazine. He described his work and asked for volunteers. Would anyone offer to help in the tagging? In answer, he received twelve replies. As time passed, though, word began to spread. The first volunteers attracted others. The others attracted still others – and publicity, too. Soon newspapers were carrying reports of the volunteers' activities. So were television and radio programs – and not surprisingly, for here was a huge mystery that needed solving, and just about anyone could take part. Eventually, the Urquharts were having their tags mass-produced, and people across the continent were applying for the chance to stick them on to monarchs . . . .

The Great Butterfly Hunt had begun.

These few words, which Urquhart included in a 1952 article on his work, began a quest that eventually involved thousands of people in Canada, Mexico, and the United States.

Marked Monarchs

Silently fluttering high above the earth, they go in search of warmer climates. Where do they go? And why? Perhaps some day we shall know the answer to the mystery of the monarch butterfly. In order to obtain sufficient information to answer the mystery of the migration of the monarchs, thousands of specimens must be tagged in as many localities as possible during the northward migration between the months of April and June and on the southward migration between August and October. It is hoped that some of the readers of this article will want to assist in the tagging and in the rearing experiments. If you want to take part in this project, address your letter to: The Royal Ontario Museum of Zoology and Palaeontology, 100 Queen's Park, Toronto 5, Ontario. Necessary labels and paper punch will be mailed to you at no cost. If enough people cooperate, we may some day be able to tell the complete story of this mysterious traveler.

NATURAL HISTORY, MAY, 1952

229

Raising Your Own

You can do more than just look at pictures of monarchs. In almost any part of the United States and southern Canada, you can raise them, too. Simply follow the instructions below when monarchs are in your region. Then get ready for an unforgettable experience as a caterpillar or chrysalis transforms before your eyes.

1

Make a rearing cage by turning a shoe box over on its end. Cut a hole in the lid (as shown) to serve as a window. Tape a sandwich wrap "curtain" over the opening. This will prevent wandering caterpillars from getting away.

2

Find an egg or caterpillar on a milkweed leaf. Don't remove it, though. Take it home with the leaf it is on and with many other leaves. You will be surprised at how many leaves one caterpillar will eat.

3

To preserve the leaves, keep their stems in water. But don't put containers of water together with the caterpillar; it could drown. Instead, before putting leaves in the cage, wrap their stems in a piece of moist paper towel. Then wrap the paper towel in sandwich wrap and secure it with a rubber band.

4

Put the leaves and the egg or caterpillar in the cage. Then watch and wait. When you have to, clean out the cage and put in more milkweed leaves.

5

When the caterpillar climbs to the top of the box and hangs down (as shown below), watch carefully! It's about to change.

About ten days later, a new butterfly will have emerged from the chrysalis. If it tried to fly indoors, it might hurt itself by banging against a window. So when it starts opening and closing its wings, take the box outside, remove the "curtain," and set the monarch free.

You could keep the monarch longer. You could feed and even tag it. But handling it can be tricky, and you need someone experienced to show you how.

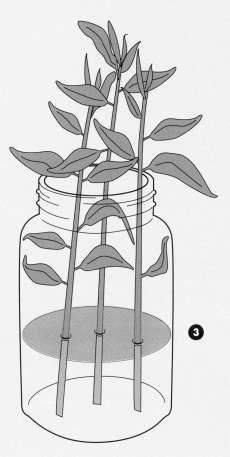

Taggers and Finders

No wonder people called this woman "the butterfly lady." With the help of her dog, Nutmeg, Ivy LeMon could tag more than 2,000 monarchs in a season. She wrote and lectured about them for more than twenty years.

With tags and homemade nets, the butterfly hunters set to work. In the southern United States, a family of four prowled the streets of their small Texas town, climbing onto roofs at five o'clock in the morning to scout the surrounding area for butterfly trees on which the roosting monarchs were still resting. In the West, a California woman led her friends on horseback over rattlesnake-infested rocks, while in the Midwest, a Michigan woman reported almost getting shot by a suspicious farmer as she pursued a specimen through his cornfield.

On the East Coast, meanwhile, people in Massachusetts were getting to know a biology teacher they called "the butterfly lady." For decades, Ivy LeMon wrote and lectured about migrating monarchs. She chased them through swamps and over barbed wire, and was known to have tagged more than two thousand specimens in a single season – although not without help. Her dog, a Brittany spaniel, would point its body in a monarch's direction, giving Ivy a chance to move in with her net.

Such enthusiasm was catching. Here, for instance, is Ivy's description of the activities of some kids in Massachusetts after she had brought word of the hunt.

"Every day during day camp at the Ipswich River Wildlife Sanctuary boys and girls tagged monarch butterflies. Campers arrived each day with shoe boxes and mason jars filled with freshly caught specimens. Many camp activities were interrupted with the cry monarch as the entire camp took off over a stone wall to retrieve one.

"Nor did this activity stop with the fall school days. Thirty-two classes were . . . briefed on the research program. Insect cages were hastily put together. Every classroom became a crawlery. Monarch larvae were feeding on tender milkweed leaves, while a student remained ready to run out for a fresh supply. . . . Escaped monarchs hung from the ceiling and walls, while teachers and principals were cheered by the class as they succeeded in catching a few.

"Finally," wrote Miss LeMon, "a cold spell ended the work for another season, but not the enthusiasm and anticipation. In every class that is visited the same question is asked. 'Have you heard if any of our monarchs made it south?'"

To get that sort of news, of course, the butterfly taggers needed butterfly finders. Would anyone notice the tagged specimens? As time passed, more and more people did. Some of the butterflies traveled first class – in boxes decorated with their favorite flowers. Others were less fortunate. One, for example, chose the wrong moment to land on a golf ball. Thwack! It went to Toronto all the same.

By throwing jeans and a jacket over his pajamas and rushing out at dawn, Mark Sandiland of Cobourg, Ontario, managed to scoop this netful of migrants out of a butterfly tree in 1972. The ninth grader got so many he had to hold some in his mouth, while transferring others to a carton. If he had visited the tree a little later, he might not have found any monarchs at all.

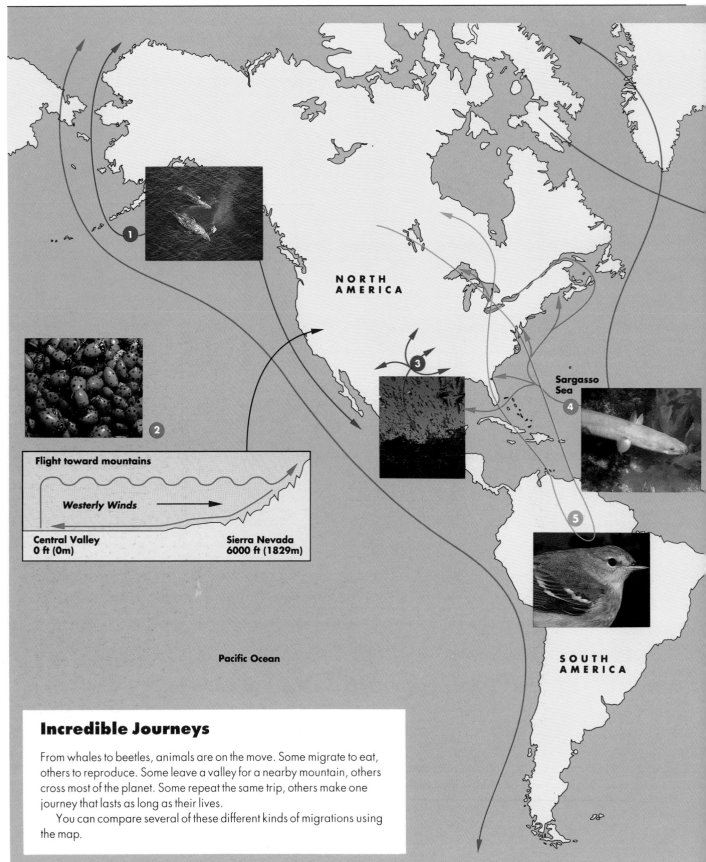

NORTH
AMERICA

Flight toward mountains

Westerly Winds

Central Valley
0 ft (0m)

Sierra Nevada
6000 ft (1829m)

Sargasso
Sea

Pacific Ocean

SOUTH
AMERICA

Incredible Journeys

From whales to beetles, animals are on the move. Some migrate to eat, others to reproduce. Some leave a valley for a nearby mountain, others cross most of the planet. Some repeat the same trip, others make one journey that lasts as long as their lives.

You can compare several of these different kinds of migrations using the map.

① Gray Whale

Leaving cold, northern waters, such as those along the coast of Alaska, gray whales begin migrating southward in late autumn – although not to feed. In fact, they may go almost completely without food for the next six months. The purpose of their two-way, 12,000-mile (19,300-km) journey: to mate or give birth. They seek lagoons along the coast of Mexico, where the warmth of the water makes it more likely that newborn whales will survive.

② Ladybird Beetle

Like some other migrants, ladybird beetles travel not north and south but up and down. When their insect food supply runs out in early summer, the ladybirds leave lush California valleys, riding air currents to cooler forests in the Sierra Nevada mountains. There they mass by the millions on logs and patches of earth. They stay inactive for six to nine months, then mate and return to the valleys. Ladybirds are, thus, one of the few insect species known to make a seasonal, two-way migration every year.

③ Mexican Free-tailed Bat

Escaping hot, dry Mexican summers, some females migrate to caves in the southern United States. There they raise so many young that Bracken Cave in Texas regularly holds some twenty million bats. Not all the bats follow this routine, though. Some stay in Mexico. Others hibernate in the United States instead of migrating back. By behaving in a variety of ways, the bats are spread around. They are therefore more likely to find the huge numbers of insects they hunt every night.

④ The American Eel

You will find it in many North American rivers – even on land, slithering between waterways. But you will never find its eggs, since it lays them in a tropical part of the Atlantic Ocean called the Sargasso Sea. For more than a year, the eel's offspring drift toward our continent. At first, they look like snippets of ribbon. Then they change into the see-through tubes, or "glass eels," sometimes found at the mouths of rivers. Afterward, they change some more. As large, yellow-brown eels, they may live twenty years in freshwater. Then, after a final transformation into silver eels, they return to their saltwater birthplace, breed, and die. Much about their lifelong migration has yet to be explained.

⑤ Blackpoll Warbler

Storing fat is an urgent chore for most migrants and especially for blackpoll warblers. These birds must eat enough to sustain them on a nonstop, 2,500-mile (4,022-km) trip over the Atlantic Ocean. Often the warblers double their weight before taking off from the northeastern United States. But sometimes they can't find enough insects to eat. When that happens, they run out of fuel partway to South America, fall into the ocean, and drown.

⑥ Arctic Tern

Crossing back and forth between its breeding grounds near the North Pole and its overwintering grounds near the South Pole, this robin-sized bird migrates farther than any other animal, traveling about twenty-five-thousand miles (or 40,022 km) each year. To do so, it will keep moving for eight months out of twelve, occasionally diving into the ocean for meals of fish.

The Map Unfolds

No matter how they arrived, however, as long as they still wore their tags, Fred Urquhart could add another pin to the large map in his office. There was already a pin that showed the place of tagging. The new one showed the place of discovery. Connected by lines of thread, the pins came to show evidence of a remarkable – in fact, an almost unbelievable – journey.

Crossing the entire eastern United States, then following the Gulf Coast, the butterflies seemed headed for Mexico! That meant they were flying more than one thousand miles (1,609 km) from their main summer homes around the Great Lakes. It was a journey longer than that of some migratory birds. And who knew where it ended? In 1964, Urquhart was describing several possibilities to his volunteers. Most likely, the monarchs roamed freely in Mexico. But perhaps they went through Mexico to its Pacific coast. Maybe they reached Central America. Or maybe they gathered elsewhere, all in one place.

As reports flowed in from taggers and finders, Fred Urquhart added migration details to a map like this one. Here each line of thread shows one butterfly's journey. A green pin shows where it was tagged; a red pin shows where it was found. By 1964, Urquhart saw that the migrants seemed headed toward Mexico. The question marks show where he thought they might finally stop.

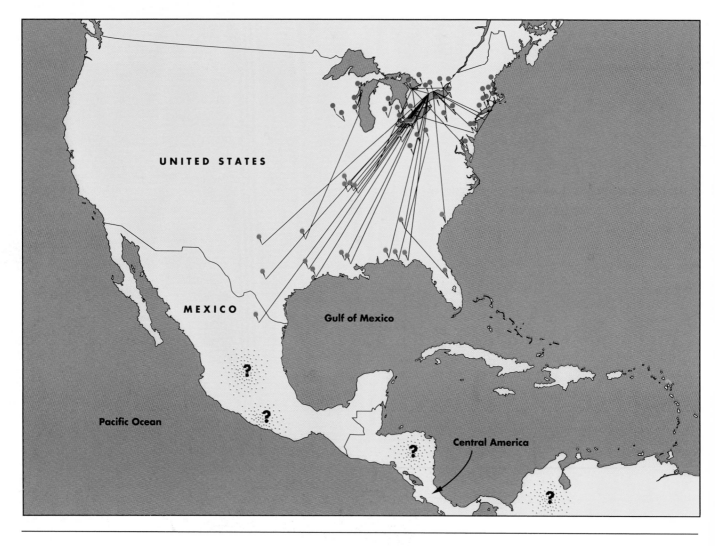

By 1964, however, a few hundred volunteers had tagged only about seventy thousand monarchs. In the end, it would take more than four hundred thousand taggings by thousands of people over a period of twenty-three years before the main part of the Great Butterfly Hunt was complete.

It would also take luck. Success depended on a few fortunate events.

A New Bermuda Triangle?

First, in 1967, the Urquharts received an invitation to spend time at a university in Texas – an invitation that gave them a priceless opportunity to hunt for monarchs. Specifically, they wanted to find butterflies that were *overwintering* – resting, in other words, after having completed the southbound part of their migration.

During the winter of 1968, Fred and Norah drove 14,000 miles (22,520 km) on this search. They followed the Rio Grande along the Mexican border, then continued through Mexico to Lake de Chapala near that country's Pacific shore. Everywhere they looked for overwintering butterflies, and everywhere they found none. In the end, Fred could only guess that the monarchs went right through Mexico to Central or even South America. However, he had shown clearly that they did not overwinter in Texas, as some people still thought they did.

Now it was a volunteer's turn to take a big step. On a car trip with his wife, Laurence Magner of Salem, Massachusetts, reached the southernmost parts of Mexico. It was winter, and he, too, looked for overwintering butterflies. He did find "resident" monarchs – monarchs that didn't migrate, that remained year-round in the warm climate of southern Mexico. But he did not find enough monarchs of any sort to account for the multitudes that people had seen pouring in from the United States. In other

It took an amateur to notice the white stripe at the top of some chrysalises – and find out what the stripe meant.

"The Best Summer of My Life"

The volunteers did much more than capture and tag monarchs. They raised, watched, and counted them. They charted their direction of flight and noted their first appearance on spring milkweed. They pushed monarch research far ahead.

The volunteers had fun, too. People who had never looked much at nature reported staying up all night to watch a caterpillar change into a chrysalis. Some became featured "monarch experts" on radio and television shows. Many young people won prizes with monarch projects, and some grew so interested in the subject they decided to become scientists. Wrote one ninth-grade tagger, "This has been the best summer of my life."

Of all these dedicated people, however, perhaps none deserves more credit than Arthur Cook of Towson, Maryland. Cook made detailed observations of the monarch's life cycle. He spent a lot of time, in other words, doing what many scientists had done before. You might have asked him: Why bother? *He* wasn't a scientist. Before he had finished, however, Cook showed everyone what a sharp-eyed amateur can do.

Cook noticed that just before a chrysalis hatched, it sometimes developed a small white stripe near its top. He then figured out that the stripe formed only if the butterfly about to emerge was a male. This was a *hypothesis*, of course – an unproven explanation. Through repeated experiments, however, Cook demonstrated that his hypothesis was true.

For this he won a national science award, or rather he won it for his school. At the time of his discovery, Arthur Cook was neither a scientist nor an adult. He was eleven years old.

words, although they had come in through the northern end of the country, they didn't seem to be coming out the southern end, or to be found anywhere in between.

So where were they?

In the newsletter he sent annually to the volunteers, Urquhart compared the mystery to that of the Bermuda Triangle, the area in the Caribbean Sea where ships and planes seem to vanish without a trace. Was a similar region swallowing butterflies in Mexico? If so, it had quite an appetite, for some 200 million monarchs were disappearing into it every year!

A Sign in a Storm

Quite a different mystery occupied an American named Kenneth Brugger as he drove home to Mexico City in the late afternoon of November 6, 1973. By then, Brugger had heard of the Great Butterfly Hunt. He had read about it in Mexico's English-language newspaper. He had even written the Urquharts offering his help as a volunteer. Nevertheless, monarchs didn't mean nearly as much to him at that moment as did Cathy Aguado, a Mexican student he had met on a vacation trip to the coastal city of Acapulco. He remembered her name and that of her town – Morelia – and had just spent

Ken Brugger, with a Mexican guide, during his search for the monarchs. Below: Part of the map Ken used in the hunt. From the spot marked "our lookout point," he and Cathy Brugger saw monarchs pouring in from the north – headed, it seemed, toward a mountain called Cerro Pelón.

the day there asking various people where she might be found.

So far no one could tell him. And now, as he drove through a range of mountains known as the Transvolcanic Belt, halfway between Morelia and Mexico City, the sky darkened and he found himself caught in a furious storm. Soon hail began to pound the roof of his motor home. He switched on his wipers, and then pulled off the road entirely. He got out of the vehicle and stood in the storm, for here was something unbelievable. It was hailing monarchs! There were thousands of them, and the road was slick with their bodies. The hail was pelting them out of the sky.

But where had they come from? Brugger recalled the newspaper article, the Urquharts' work . . . and then, all at once, he knew. He just *knew* that the key to the mystery must be somewhere nearby.

The Bruggers trekked repeatedly through the thick, steeply sloped forests of south-central Mexico. "There were rock slides," says Ken. "There were also people slides." In this picture, they have strapped ropes to a horse, which is pulling Cathy along.

It was; and so, as it happened, was Cathy. Not only did Brugger find her, he convinced her to marry him, and then discovered that they shared a common interest . . . in butterflies. How extraordinary. In finding Cathy, Ken had gained a partner in the quest.

In fact, Cathy seemed to be the perfect partner. As a girl she had learned to find her way through the thick mountain forests of the region. She could speak with the local people not only in Spanish but also in their own Indian dialect. Together, thought Ken, they would make an ideal butterfly-hunting team.

And so they did. Soon Ken and Cathy were making trip after trip to the region of the butterfly hail. They hunted down monarchs, took pictures, and mailed report after report back to the Urquharts. They also mailed sample monarchs. True, they did not come across any more huge throngs of butterflies such as Ken had seen in the storm. Nevertheless, some of their samples turned out to be migrants. With growing excitement, Fred Urquhart urged the Bruggers on.

Across the continent meanwhile, butterfly hunters were tearing open their newsletters to read a wonderful announcement. Due to the efforts of one Kenneth Brugger, the butterfly mystery was almost solved! It was the spring of 1974. By fall, the Urquharts had hired the Bruggers to hunt butterflies full-time.

Closing In

This meant crossing the countryside week after week – sometimes in Ken's motor home, sometimes by motorcycle, most often on foot. During the day they visited poor, dusty towns, where Cathy questioned the people about the clouds of butterflies that sometimes passed overhead. Then at night she and Ken compared the people's observations with their own, for by now, they, too, were seeing the clouds of monarchs pouring in through mountain passes and along river valleys to the north.

Eventually, the search led to Cerro Pelón, a mountain more than two and one-half miles (4 km) high, whose forested slopes give way to a bare rock outcropping at the top.

Eventually, their search led them to Cerro Pelón. It was a 2½-mile- (4-km-) high mountain whose full name means "bald mountain," since its forested slopes give way to a bare rock outcropping at the top. Were the monarchs on Cerro Pelón? There was only one way to find out. With the help of a guide and his horse (and with the constant companionship of their dog, Kola), the Bruggers began to climb. Day after day, they scaled Cerro Pelón. They would start early in the morning and return to the motor home well after dusk. Each time, they chose a new route to the top.

No matter how they approached the mountain, however, Ken and Cathy first had to walk through a patchwork of farms and villages that circled its base. And, unfortunately, not everyone in these places was happy to see them. There were armed men about, who doubted their story of missing butterflies and who accused them of seeking treasure or minerals to which a foreigner like Ken had no right. The couple was threatened repeatedly. And they frequently had to cross bare patches of hillside on which they could be easily seen, or even shot! Afraid for their lives, they nonetheless continued to climb.

Finally, around daybreak one morning, Ken saw a single monarch skimming down the mountain's western face. Where had it come from? It wouldn't fly at night, of course, so there could only be one answer: It came from the top. But from where at the top? Keeping its flight path in mind, the Bruggers began to climb once again. After a while, they had other clues to help them – the remains of dead monarchs. These monarchs had been killed by birds and mice, and now their wings and bodies littered the ground. The wings and bodies formed a trail. The trail led almost to the summit, then veered off into a thick and dark forest.

And it was there, on January 2, 1975, that Ken and Cathy Brugger found the butterflies – not hundreds or thousands or tens of thousands of butterflies, but *tens of millions*. There were so many monarchs hanging from the trees, that thick branches were sagging and thinner ones were even snapping under their weight.

Most of the time the migrants hung motionless, their closed wings covering the trees almost to their topmost branches in a dull, brownish drapery. But as the sun shone into the grove, the Bruggers saw some of the monarchs slowly open their wings and take briefly to flight. Then, gradually, the colony awakened until, at last, butterfly rivers cascaded along the forest floor while orange clouds billowed above orange trees.

Says Cathy, "I could not speak. I was just frozen and my heart was beating so fast. . . . What a marvelous thing this was. And I wished, at that moment, that all people could feel what I was feeling: the magnificence of the butterflies."

▶
Led on by a trail of wings, the Bruggers reached their goal. Some two miles (3 km) up Cerro Pelón, they found countless monarchs blanketing the forest. The butterflies covered Cathy, too, as she stood among the trees.

Butterfly Treasure

John McClusky (left) with his family and Cathy Brugger (far right). The Bruggers visited the McCluskys at their home in Fredericksburg, Texas, after the discovery of John's homemade tag (above).

"I've always wanted to find things, to discover things," says John McClusky. Nowadays, for John, that means studying molecules as a research chemist near Houston, Texas. Back in 1974, however, when he was thirteen, it meant tagging monarch butterflies in his hometown of Fredericksburg, Texas. Other kids made fun of this skinny, bookish boy who loved science and who bicycled around with his net. In fact, some adults might have made fun of him, too, because what John McClusky was doing seemed entirely absurd.

With only an old book to guide him, John was trying to solve the monarch mystery – all by himself. True, the book was Fred Urquhart's. But it was fourteen years old. "For all I knew, Urquhart had retired," he explains. John had no idea that people all over the country were tagging monarchs in a standard, time-tested way. So, instead, he bought ordinary address labels at a local dime store, hand-lettered them in India ink, and attached them in an outdated way that Urquhart mentioned in the book. He didn't attach very many, either. Other taggers knew of butterfly trees; they tagged thousands in a season. They had been doing this every year since before John was born. But John knew of no butterfly trees. So he tagged one hundred monarchs – as many as he could capture pedaling around town.

How strange, then, how incredibly improbable, that it was one of John McClusky's butterflies that ended up at Ken Brugger's feet!

To have found any tagged monarch would have been unusual enough. Just ask the scientist who has spent more time than any other among the overwintering butterflies. William Calvert reports finding just one such specimen in thirteen years of research. But Brugger found McClusky's label almost at once. It was an oddball, all right. Yet it served a huge purpose, for it was the first item of evidence that proved the butterflies which massed in Mexico were the same butterflies which migrated through Canada and the United States.

Since then, scientists have learned a great deal more about the eastern monarch's journey. Their research has shown, for instance, that the butterflies do more, much more, than fly south to some broad, general area. Rather, they home in on a single, small region some seventy-five miles

The mystery solved. Twenty-three years after the Great Butterfly Hunt began, scientists could finally draw a map like this one. As shown, monarchs east of the Rocky Mountains migrate to one small region of Mexico. To do so they fly an average of 1,800 miles (2,900 km). Many make a crossing of the entire United States.

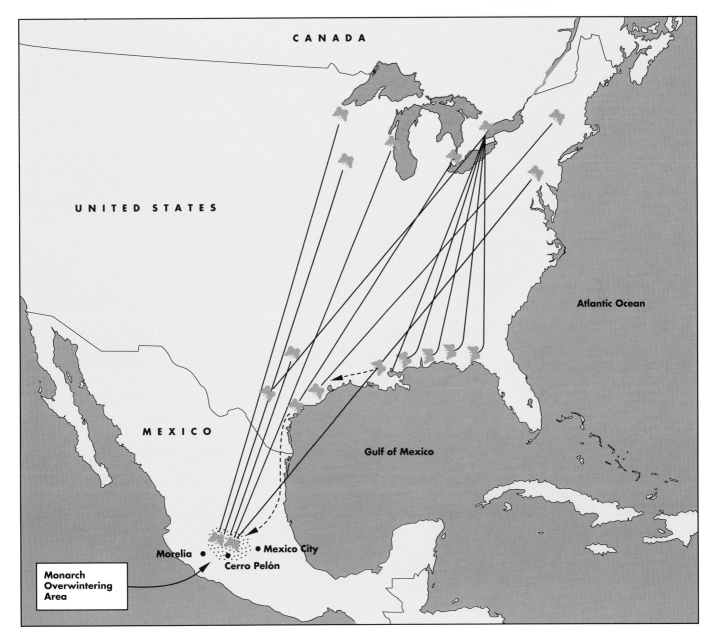

CANADA

UNITED STATES

Atlantic Ocean

MEXICO

Gulf of Mexico

Morelia ●

● Mexico City

Cerro Pelón

Monarch
Overwintering
Area

Monarchs almost entirely coat the trees in their overwintering places. They cling to trunks, branches, leaves, and each other. By avoiding the bottommost and topmost parts of the trees, they escape killing cold, hungry mice, and lashing winds.

(120 km) long by thirty-five miles (56 km) wide. And even within this region you might never see one, since their final stopping points are even more specific. They form colonies in tiny groves of forest ranging from the size of a baseball diamond to that of a large city block. The Bruggers had found only the first of all these places on January 2, 1975. It took years for them and other explorers to discover the rest. We now know that during an average winter, the region plays host to about nine such colonies in all.

Towers and Clusters

The butterflies, by contrast, seem to have no difficulty in finding their overwintering groves, or the region that holds them. Starting in early November, they pour in through mountain passes and river valleys to the north. Flying about a crow's-length apart, they form complicated patterns against the sky. What do the patterns mean? To this day, no one knows. And what does it mean when they rise up in huge spiraling towers above some ridges? These towers are so high that, even with binoculars, watchers cannot see their tops. Are the towers beacons? No one knows that, either. By early December, however, the towers disappear, and the monarchs crowd together in stands of trees along the slopes. Then, gradually, they shift position until they finally come to rest – usually at the heads of valleys, usually near water, and usually within two-thirds of a mile (1 km) of the place where monarchs overwintered the previous year.

The Mexican colonies. About nine monarch colonies form every winter in the oyamel forests of south-central Mexico. Each colony sits on the cool heights of a mountain about 10,000 feet (3 km) above sea level. Most form at the heads of valleys, near water. Usually they turn up within two-thirds of a mile (1 km) of where monarchs overwintered the previous year.

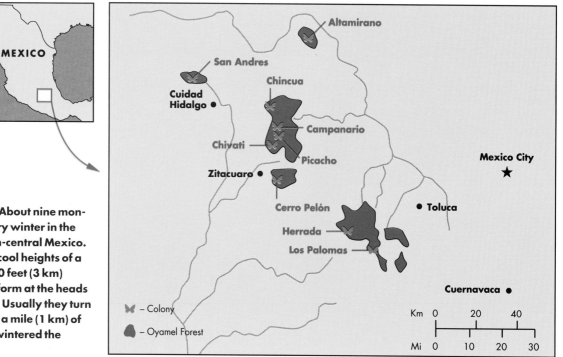

Somehow they choose these sites. Then they pour into them, covering pines and cedars, but mainly *oyamel* trees on whose needlelike leaves the tiny hooks on their legs more readily cling. You cannot see much of an oyamel once the butterflies have landed on it – only the bottommost stretch of trunk and the topmost triangle of branches. The rest is covered with migrants. In clumps and clusters they may form a winged coat up to fifty feet (15 m) long. And there they hang. In the summer, you would have had a hard time even approaching a monarch. It would have spotted you quickly and bolted away. But now you can pick one right out of a cluster, and it will just lie there, paralyzed by cold, for it has chosen to overwinter some two miles (3 km) above sea level. And at such heights, even in Mexico, temperatures stay mainly below the fifty-five degree Farenheit (13°C) point at which monarchs can fly.

Monarch Honor Roll

John McClusky was not the only teenager to make history during the Great Butterfly Hunt. On September 6, 1975, Jim Street and Dean Boen, both junior high school students in Chaska, Minnesota, set in motion an amazing coincidence.

As they had done many times that summer, the boys spent the day tagging monarchs. At some point they attached tag number ps 397 to a migrant they found sipping nectar in a field.

That winter, Fred Urquhart made his first trip to see the Mexican overwintering places. He spent several days in one particular colony. Then, on his last day there, he sat down amid a pile of fallen butterflies to have his picture taken. Reaching into the pile, he picked one out. The butterfly was ps 397! Against all odds, it wore Jim and Dean's tag.

The tag proved, of course, that monarchs reach Mexico from Minnesota. But it meant far more to Urquhart. For it was his own creation, a symbol of his success. And he called finding it the most exciting experience of his career.

Dean Boen (center) and Jim Street with their teacher, Jim Gilbert, on the day they labeled ps 397.

Against all odds, Fred Urquhart picks a tagged butterfly – ps 397 – out of a pile of thousands during his first trip to see the Mexican migrants. Urquhart later described this moment as the most exciting of his career.

Storms come rarely to the monarch colonies, but when they do they may kill millions of migrants. In this picture, for example, the butterflies have been knocked to the ground by snow. Are they dead? Most likely. But some, warmed by the sun, may yet return to the trees.

Only on warmer days can they peel themselves from their hanging places, and only then do they fill the sky like a million living sparkles, drifting into the valleys to sip nectar from wild flowers and water from streams. The rest of the time they are helpless. When the trees shake, it rains monarchs. After storms, you can find yourself ankle-deep in butterflies. They die by the millions – victims of cold, hunger, thirst, smoke, birds. . . . Scientists estimate that in an average year, starvation alone kills one migrant out of every five.

Strange as it may seem, however, scientists now believe that these mountaintop groves are the best places for overwintering monarchs. Why? Because the butterflies, while cold, are not too cold. Temperatures in the groves stay above the freezing point most of the time. At the same time, the migrants are not so warm that they flutter around constantly, burning up vital stores of fat. That would be disastrous, for their work is not done. Flying south is only the beginning. With the lengthening days of February and March, nature issues new commands. "Now you must mate," she seems to instruct the monarchs. "Then, you must fly north again."

For this they need all the fat they can store. They need it to burn as fuel. If you visit a colony at the end of March, you will get some idea of just how much fuel they need. You will find the migrants in a swarming, mating frenzy, as millions of males chase millions of females among the trees. A few days later, though, only a scattering of butterflies lingers on. The rest are on their way north again. They are flying through the mountain passes, through the river valleys – back the way they came.

The Monarch-Milkweed Connection

Does all milkweed look alike?

In Mexico some grow in deserts and look like miniature Christmas trees while in the eastern United States some grow in marshes and look like bushes. In Arizona some coil around bushes (they look like vines) while on certain Caribbean islands some have seed pods like melons and grow nine feet (3 m) high.

From Michigan: Butterfly weed, a kind of milkweed.

Whatever their shape, size, or color, however, the different species of milkweed still attract the egg-laying monarch female.

Even if they are the newest of growths – tiny, hidden by other plants – she finds them. She sees them with her eyes, smells them with her antennae, and finally tastes them with special sensors on her feet. All in all, scientists have counted some two thousand different species of milkweed in the world. But of the hundred or so in North America, the scientists suggest that only a

The Clock Starts

But back to *where*? For decades, the Urquharts and their fellow taggers have tried to solve this mystery, too. In this case, however, the task has proven more difficult. For one thing, the returning migrants don't bunch together. Instead, they fan out across the south-central and southeastern United States. For another, they're hard to catch. Why? Because they rarely stop, even to eat. They can't stop. They have no time. At the moment they became capable of mating, the migrants' extra-long youth ended. Now, like summer monarchs, they have about a month to live.

Perhaps someday you will see a returning female migrant struggling through her last minutes. Tattered and exhausted, she flits clumsily from one milkweed leaf to another, laying a single jewel-like egg on each. In the end, she may have covered 4,000 miles (6,436 km) and laid some six hundred eggs.

How far *do* the returning migrants travel? Scientists are not sure. One monarch which may have been tagged in Mexico, was seen, though not captured, in Maple Springs, New York. And perhaps the eggs of a few such hardy specimens do indeed hatch into all the northern monarchs we see. However, scientists at the University of Florida think not. And they have developed a remarkable way of backing up this belief. You could say they have discovered a new kind of tag.

Like mirror images, these monarch couples mate. With spring come profound changes in the migrants. For as they become capable of reproducing, they begin to age, and die within about a month of leaving the mountaintop groves.

few have led the monarch so far from its tropical home.

Today milkweed appears as far from the tropics as Canada, but that has not always been the case. Millions of years ago, all milkweed, along with all monarchs, lived in the hot and wet regions of North, Central, and South America. Gradually, however, milkweed began to spread. Certain species crept northward, developing new shapes and patterns of growth suited to the conditions they found.

Meanwhile, in northeastern Mexico, monarchs were facing a problem – dry winters during which the milkweed and other plants they relied on withered and died. To survive in these places, the monarchs, too, had to change.

And so they did. Over thousands or even millions of years, they developed a new way of living. During the winter months, they stopped breeding, aging, or even moving. They became "semi-dormant." In this way, they reduced their need for scarce supplies of food. They could also take advantage of the more northerly milkweed – they could fly off to find it each spring as long as they returned each autumn to the warmer climate of Mexico. There, in remote forests they could survive until the following spring by falling into their energy-saving, semi-dormant state.

Is this really how monarch migration began? Some scientists speculate that it is. They believe it took its present form about ten thousand years ago, at the end of the last ice age. Even so, they have no proof. They cannot explain the steps by which an insect would have evolved such a complicated pattern of behavior. A speculation, of course, is merely an educated guess.

The Tag Within

There's no need to attach this one, though. For this tag is a chemical. Called a *cardenolide*, it's found in milkweed and gets into the body of the monarch caterpillar through the milkweed the caterpillar eats. Nor can this tag fall off. It remains permanently in the caterpillar, the chrysalis, and the adult butterfly, too. Furthermore, it's a tag that needs no serial number, since its ingredients reveal the location from which it has come.

Suppose, then, that you wanted to find out the birthplace of the adult monarchs that first appear in springtime in the northern United States. By analyzing the cardenolides in the bodies of these monarchs, you would discover which species of milkweed they had eaten as caterpillars. Then, by looking up where the species grows, you could figure out where the butterflies had hatched.

In fact, this is exactly what the Florida scientists have done. They have examined some of the earliest northern monarchs. And the result? They discovered that the monarchs had hatched only weeks before, on a milkweed species that grows in springtime, in the southern United States. The monarchs, in other words, were the offspring of the returning Mexican migrants that had laid their eggs in Texas, Louisiana, Alabama. . . . They had never been to Mexico themselves.

It appears, then, that returning Mexican migrants do not make a complete round trip. Instead, they leave it to the next generation to reach the monarch species' northernmost homes. But if that's so, then this next generation must also be a generation of migrants, specially programmed for travel. Does this mean that they also live extra-long lives? That they home in on a particular location? That they follow certain routes?

So far, no one knows. By trying to answer some questions about the monarch, it seems we have uncovered a swarm of new ones.

And above all these stands the biggest mystery of all.

Chemicals called cardenolides, taken from the bodies of various monarchs, form patterns of spots in this experiment. The patterns reveal which species of milkweed the cardenolides originally came from. Since different milkweed species grow in different places, the experiment shows scientists where each monarch began its life.

Delicious or Deadly?

"Look!" someone says. But the frog blends in so well with the lily pad it's almost impossible to see.

It is quite easy to understand, however, why so many animals take on the colors and textures of their environment. Monarchs, by contrast, seem not to care about standing out, and you might well wonder why some sharp-eyed, insect-eating birds don't finish off entire colonies of monarchs in a few gigantic feasts.

You would not be the first to wonder about this. In fact, naturalists of the last century came up with a theory to explain why some creatures are so brilliantly colored. The colors, they theorized, warn potential enemies to stay away. Consider such eye-catching forms of wildlife as honeybees, yellow jackets, and coral snakes, for example, and you will see that most carry weapons which make them a

Two species, two ways of surviving. The comma butterfly blends in, the viceroy stands out.

poor choice as a meal.

As for monarchs, they may seem harmless; nevertheless, they may fit the theory perfectly, because they eat cardenolides, those milkweed chemicals described on the facing page. Cardenolides, say many scientists, will poison almost any creature that might try to eat a monarch.

To prove this, Professor Lincoln Brower, a well-known researcher at the University of Florida, put monarchs and blue jays together. The hungry jays, having never seen this kind of insect before, readily attacked. But after sampling a monarch with its ingested cardenolides, they threw up and never bothered one again.

In fact, birds find monarchs so unpleasant that, according to Brower and others, they won't even pursue anything that *looks* like one. This has allowed another species of butterfly to take advantage of the monarch-milkweed relationship. The viceroy butterfly eats no milkweed so contains no cardenolides. But it has evolved to look almost exactly like the monarch, and lives in safety as a result.

Or so almost everyone says. Fred Urquhart disagrees. He does not believe monarchs are poisonous. Nor does he believe that viceroys mimic monarchs. And he tells of another experiment in which caged starlings stayed perfectly healthy while eating monarchs – cardenolides and all.

The biggest challenge to the idea of poisonous monarchs, however, comes not from experiments but from Mexico, where, over the course of a winter, birds may eat two million monarchs in one colony alone.

How does Brower explain it? For one thing, he says, most Mexican migrants come from places where they feed on less poisonous or nonpoisonous milkweeds. For another, the monarch-eating birds belong to only two species, which have learned to resist the poison or pick it away.

So who is right, Urquhart or Brower? Urquhart? Then how do monarchs get away with showing off those spectacular wings?

The Biggest Mystery of All

How do the migrants find their way?

How, for instance, do monarchs from Minnesota stay on course for weeks over fields, cities, mountains, and deserts until they finally reach those tiny patches of Mexican forest? Well, they clearly need a built-in sense of direction. But is that enough? Obviously not, because monarchs from New Hampshire must head in an entirely different direction from the Minnesota butterflies. Yet they reach the groves all the same.

So, too, arctic terns, Mexican free-tailed bats, American eels, and all the other long-range migrants need not only a sense of direction but also a sense of place. In order to know how to proceed, they need to know where they are. Like hearing and sight, such senses have evolved over millions of years. Only since 1950, however, have people begun to understand what these direction-finding and place-finding tools might be.

That was the year two German scientists discovered the sun-compass. Gustav Kramer discovered it in birds, Karl von Frisch in honeybees. Since then, others have found it in lizards, turtles, snakes, and other creatures. To stay headed in a certain direction, these animals keep themselves in a given position relative to the sun.

Opposite:
As winter ends, monarchs pour out of a colony, abandoning it completely in a matter of days.

The Lost Ones

"We were five days or 1,000 miles from New York when we ran through a massive swarm of monarch butterflies."

So wrote a sailor named Vincent Varey aboard ship in the Atlantic Ocean in September 1944. After his vessel survived a hurricane, Varey was surprised to find thousands of monarchs trying to gain a foothold on the rigging and fluttering about the decks. He would have been even more surprised had he known where those monarchs were *supposed* to be.

Monarchs do try to correct themselves if blown off course. In strong winds, however, they may get blown off course for good – in which case they may end up in the midst of the Atlantic Ocean, in Florida, or on islands in the Caribbean Sea. Frequently, they arrive in the Yucatan Peninsula of Mexico. Fred Urquhart suggests that they travel even farther southward than that, to the country of Guatemala. There, perhaps, they form overwintering colonies that have yet to be found.

Monarchs are not the only creatures to lose their way. For unknown reasons, some birds and other migrants will wander off course, even in perfect weather, and may end up headed in precisely the opposite direction from the rest of their kind.

Usually such creatures perish, but sometimes they become pioneers, introducing their species into the places where they come to rest.

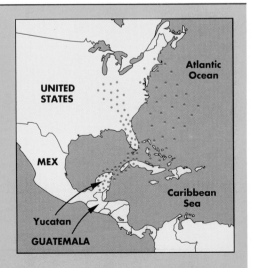

Off-course monarchs: The dots show where they may appear.

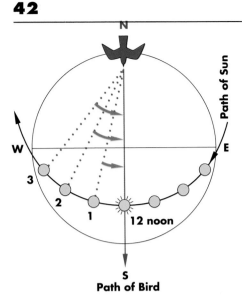

How do birds tell direction? Like many animals, they use the sun as a compass. To keep on heading south, the bird in this diagram, for example, flies toward a point farther and farther to the east of the setting sun. To do so, of course, it needs a keen sense of time.

To fly south, for example, a robin will head directly toward the sun at noon, when the sun has reached the halfway point in its east-to-west journey across the sky. The robin will keep a little to the east of the sun at one o'clock, a little farther east of the sun at two o'clock, and so on, thus maintaining its southward bearing at all times.

Could a monarch behave similarly? To do so, it would need a built-in clock. Lots of animals have those. But keep in mind that monarchs stay on course, veering neither to the east nor to the west, even when they cannot see the sun. So, while they might use a sun-compass, they must also have another means of finding their way.

By now, scientists have uncovered a whole list of alternative methods. They have found, for example, that some migrants use the stars as a compass. Some seek out landmarks, listen for the sound of the sea, or even sniff the air for the familiar smell of home.

As it happens, though, none of these methods could possibly explain monarch navigation. Since some monarchs never approach the sea, how can they listen for waves? Since they make their trips only once, how can they learn to recognize landmarks? And since they leave no scent on the butterfly trees, what can they possibly smell?

The Best Guess

In fact, scientists have no certain idea how the monarch performs its navigational feats. But they do have a favorite guess. Strange as it may seem, they suggest that the roaming butterflies actually sense tiny changes in the earth's magnetic field.

It is certainly difficult to think of any animal sensing the force that causes the needles on human-made compasses to point north and south. The magnetic field of the earth is extremely weak – several hundred times weaker than the magnet on the average refrigerator door. Nevertheless, an ordinary compass can detect the field at any location on the planet, by day or by night, in any weather. And an instrument that's even more sensitive can use the field to tell not only direction but also location. How? By sensing the angle and strength of the field. As you can see in the diagram on page 43, the angle and strength of the earth's magnetic field change as you move from the equator toward a pole.

Could a living being develop such a keenly sensitive instrument? For a long time researchers dismissed the idea as impossible. In the early 1970s, however, experiments conducted in New York State revealed that pigeons may possess just such a device.

As any reader of history books knows, pigeons are champion navigators. They have linked together empires by carrying messages vast distances to their nests. To navigate, they use the sun, landmarks, and perhaps other clues. And yet, even on the cloudiest of days, even blind, a pigeon can find its nest many miles or kilometers away.

Finding Your Way in a Magnetic Field

To see a magnetic field in action, move a compass in a circle around a bar magnet. You will find the compass's needle pointing toward the bar magnet at different angles, depending on where the compass is placed. Actually, the needle is lining up with the bar's magnetic field.

You can think of the bar's magnetic field as being made up of imaginary lines, called *flux lines*, that curve from one end of the magnet to the other – from its north pole to its south pole. You can think of the earth's magnetic field in the same way. (In fact, you can think of the earth as a ball with a kind of bar magnet poked through its center!) At any point along a flux line, the line curves at a certain angle – it has a certain strength. As a result, if you can detect differences in a flux line's angle or strength, you can tell how far north you are in the magnetic field, or how far south.

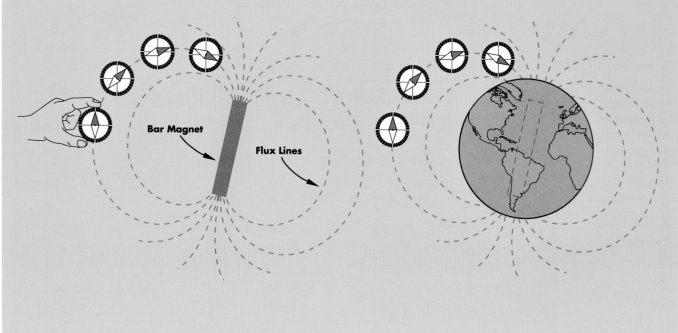

Bar Magnet

Flux Lines

By placing electric coils on the heads of pigeons like this one, scientists have tried to prove that the birds navigate by sensing the earth's magnetic field. The coils distort the field over a small area. Do they confuse the pigeons? According to some researchers, the coil-carrying pigeons head in the opposite direction of home.

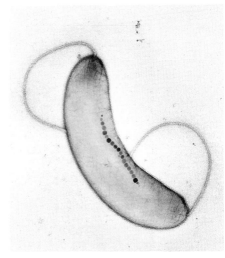

While pigeons may respond to the earth's magnetic field, scientists have no doubt that this microscopic bacterium does. You can even see the magnetite particles lined up in its body. They make the microscopic creature act just like a compass needle. Even dead, its body points north and south.

You might therefore speculate that pigeons navigate by sensing the earth's magnetic field. To test this hypothesis, the New York researchers strapped electric coils to the heads of several pigeons on a cloudy day when the birds would have no other clues to guide them. The coils generated a magnetic field that distorted the earth's magnetic field around the pigeon's heads. The result? According to the researchers, the pigeons couldn't find their way home, and flew in exactly the opposite direction.

What's more, scientists have found tiny specks of a magnetic material, called *magnetite*, in all sorts of creatures – in some microscopic ocean-dwelling bacteria, for example, in pigeons and bats, and, yes, even in monarch butterflies. In the bacteria, the magnetite particles line up with the magnetic field of the earth, thus pointing the bacteria toward the nearest pole and also downward toward the ocean bottom in the regions where they live.

This suggests that larger animals might also use the magnetite particles to find their way. It is not yet clear, however, whether the particles form part of any organ or attach to any nerves. So how might these animals obtain any information from them? So far, no one knows.

In fact, it may be that the magnetite serves no purpose, and monarchs are completely unable to sense magnetic forces. Researchers must still prove otherwise. They have yet to take the first steps in explaining monarch navigation. And they had better get moving. Otherwise, they may never have the chance to try.

A Twenty-Year Deadline?

For you see, even as the research into monarch migration continues, the migrants themselves may be disappearing. Just ask Lincoln Brower, one of the world's foremost monarch researchers. According to Brower, the migrants may be gone completely in less than twenty years.

You can already see evidence of their disappearance. You can see it in a few of the Mexican overwintering areas where workers have invaded and cut down trees. You can see it in parts of California, where land developers have cleared away groves to make room for houses. And you can see it throughout the United States and southern Canada – in your own neighborhood, perhaps – where local officials have sprayed poisonous chemicals on roadsides and fields. The chemicals get rid of unwanted plants. The plants include milkweed. As a result, the monarchs have fewer wild flowers from which to drink nectar, and fewer leaves on which to lay eggs.

As a result, there may soon be many fewer monarchs. But there are more people than ever before. In south-central Mexico especially, the human population has boomed. The people need lumber and firewood. To get it, they are advancing ever higher into the mountains of the Transvolcanic Belt. Only rarely have they actually entered a colony, but in thinning out the surrounding forests they threaten the migrants just the same.

With the forest thinned, the monarchs no longer have the insulating blanket of trees that once protected them from drying winds and lashing storms. Furthermore, the average temperature drops. Most likely, the temperature drops only a few degrees. Nevertheless, those few degrees can mean life or death for millions of monarchs.

Rarely have Mexican woodcutters actually cut down trees in the monarchs' overwintering places. But in thinning out the surrounding forests, as shown here, they threaten the migrants just the same.

Save the Butterflies!

So what can people who care about the monarchs do – demand that the Mexicans not cut so much wood? In 1986, the government of Mexico did exactly that. It passed laws protecting large areas of trees. Such laws, if followed, would protect many of the overwintering areas. The people who live near these areas are extremely poor, however. Wood-cutting is one of their best ways of making money. They need the trees to live.

With this in mind, members of a Mexican organization called Monarca A.C. have come up with a new approach. Instead of simply telling the people not to cut down trees, Monarca is helping them make a different kind of living from their environment – by breeding fish, for example, or by growing flowers and fruit. Monarca is even helping them profit from the migrants themselves. With help and encouragement from Monarca, local people are now providing food, souvenirs, and guided trips into the mountains to the thousands of visitors who come to see the butterflies every year.

In California, meanwhile, an organization called the Xerces Society is urging politicians, real estate developers, and landowners to protect the famous butterflies of the Pacific coast.

Regrettably, not everyone reports these efforts a success. In Mexico, some say lumbering continues both in and around various overwintering areas. And some say that all the tourism and new projects benefit only a

Going, Going, Gone?

Given all the threats facing the monarch butterfly, you might think of it as a species at risk of disappearing – in other words, an endangered species like the peregrine falcon and the African elephant.

But is it really? Not at all. Even the total destruction of the overwintering colonies in Mexico and California would leave many monarchs thriving in places like

southern Mexico, Central America, South America, Australia, and on islands in the Pacific Ocean and the Caribbean Sea.

For the time being, then, the only thing that may vanish is the monarch's migration and, along with it, the chance to marvel at it, to study it, and to learn how it evolved.

A migration is not a species, of course. It is, rather, a *phenomenon* – something that happens. Is a phenomenon worth saving? For a long time, this question entered few people's minds. We have, after all, so many disappearing species to worry about. But recently, some researchers have begun paying attention to disappearing phenomena, too.

In fact, a major conservation association has for the first time included an endangered phenomenon on its list of endangered species. The phenomenon listed: monarch migration. It is not, however, the only one.

In the Canadian town of Inwood,

Manitoba, for instance, you might wake up on an average September morning to find snakes in your kitchen, snakes in your basement, and snakes by the hundreds slithering through your yard! Migrating across large stretches of land and water, the reptiles finally reach underground dens, where they cram themselves together – as many as twelve thousand per den – until warm weather returns.

Does this description sound familiar? Like the monarchs, every autumn the harmless snakes home in on the same tiny territories. Like the monarchs, they begin the spring in a mating frenzy. And like the monarchs, their numbers are shrinking. Local snake pickers are selling them by the thousands to pet stores and scientific labs.

Will we therefore run out of red-sided garter snakes? Not at all. The pickers don't bother chasing down every last one. But the amazing phenomenon of their mass migration, like that of the monarch, may soon disappear.

few people, while leaving the rest just as poor as before, and just as much in need of wood and land.

Suppose, however, that the Bruggers had never found the colonies. Suppose that the Urquharts had never launched their quest. The people of south-central Mexico would still have multiplied. They would still need trees. Only in this case, no one would have even tried to stop the destruction of the forests. No one would have known, perhaps ever, why this destruction should be stopped.

If Monarca does succeed, then, it will have a special group of people to thank: The Great Butterfly Hunters – Fred and Norah Urquhart, Ken and Cathy Brugger, Ivy LeMon in Massachusetts, John McClusky in Texas . . . thousands of others. Through years of effort, these people may have done far more than discover where the monarchs of eastern North America spend the winter. In finding them, they may have saved them, too.

"Protected Area. Monarch Butterflies." While signs like this one announce that the butterflies enjoy government protection, more than signs are required to save the migrants. A conservation group is trying to help people near the colonies make more money from tourism than from wood.

See for Yourself

For information about visiting the overwintering colonies, write to:

Dr. William Calvert
503 East Mary Street
Austin, Texas
78704

48

Index

Credits

Photos: Front cover Stephen Dalton, Animals Animals **Back cover** Albert Moldvay , Eriako Associates **1** Dwight R. Kuhn **2-3** George D. Lepp, Comstock **5** Frans Lanting, Minden Pictures **6** Jack Couffer, Bruce Coleman Inc. **7** E.R. Degginger, Animals, Animals **8** (both) Jeff Foott **9** David C. Fritts, Animals, Animals **10** (top) Jeff Foott; (bottom) Donald Specker, Animals, Animals **11** Erik Christensen, The Globe and Mail, Toronto **12-13** (bottom, left to right) ① Dick Poe, Visuals Unlimited; ② John H. Gerard, Bruce Coleman Inc.; ③ Frans Lanting, Minden Pictures; ④-⑦ John Shaw; ⑧ John Shaw, Tom Stack & Associates, **13** (top) L. West, The National Audubon Society Collection, Photo Researchers **14-15** (bottom) Dr. A.C. Twomey, The National Audubon Society Collection, Photo Researchers; (top) George D. Lepp, Bio-Tec Images **16** Harry N. Darrow, Bruce Coleman Inc. **17** Jeff Foott, Bruce Coleman Inc. **18** (left) James R. Larison; (bottom) NASA **19** Jeff Foott, Bruce Coleman Inc. **22** (top) Jack Woolner, Fish and Game Department, Estate of Ivy LeMon; (center) Estate of Ivy LeMon **23** courtesy Audrey Wilson **24-25** ① Francois Gohier; ② Don & Esther Phillips, Tom Stack & Associates; ③ Stephen Krasemann, The National Audubon Society Collection, Photo Researchers; ④ Harold Wes Pratt; ⑤ Patti Murray, Animals, Animals; ⑥ Gordon Langsbury, Bruce Coleman Inc. **27** Muriel Williams, Photo/Nats **28** (both) Albert Moldvay, Eriako Associates **29** Kenneth C. Brugger **30-31** (both) Albert Moldvay, Eriako Associates **32** (top) Kenneth C. Brugger; (tag) courtesy Lois McClusky **34** George D. Lepp, Comstock **35** (left) Bianca Lavies © 1976 National Geographic Society; (right) David Gilbert, courtesy Jim Gilbert **36** (top) William H. Calvert (bottom) John Gerlach, Visuals Unlimited **37** William H. Calvert **38** Lincoln P. Brower **39** (bottom) John Shaw; (inset) Breck P. Kent, Animals, Animals **41** Lincoln P. Brower **44** (top) Russ Charif; (center) R. Blakemore, N. Blakemore **45** George D. Lepp, Bio-Tec Images **46** Francois Gohier **47** (both) Frans Lanting, Minden Pictures

Maps/illustrations: Matthew Bartholomew. Produced by WGBH Publishing and Design.

Portions of this book appeared previously in *Newscience*, published by the Ontario Science Centre. Excerpt on p. 20 from "Marked Monarchs," by Fred A. Urquhart, extracted from *Natural History*, May, 1952. Excerpt on p. 22 by Ivy LeMon, from *Insect Migration Studies*, reprinted by permission of Fred A. Urquhart and Shirley Duffy.

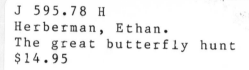

DISCARD